Smallfellow Press

A Division of Tallfellow Press, Inc. and
Every Picture Tells A Story..., Inc.
1180 South Beverly Drive Los Angeles, California 90035

Library of Congress catalog-in-publishing data in progress
RIP SQUEAK™ is a trademark of Leonard Filgate

ISBN 1-931290-01-6

First Edition - First Printing
Printed in Italy

www.Ripsqueak.com

You can find the art of Leonard Filgate and many other illustrators at:
everypicture.com

Rip Squeak and His Friends

Illustrated by Leonard Filgate
Written by Susan Yost-Filgate

For Jessica

Smallfellow Press

One morning the humans left the cottage, taking their suitcases with them. The house was soooo quiet.

Rip Squeak sat at his desk daydreaming about great adventures. He would occasionally scribble a thought, but soon the sweet aroma of cinnamon tickled his nose and made his stomach growl. He followed the sugary smell into the hall where he found his sister Jesse. Together they tiptoed towards the kitchen.

"Are you sure all the cats went too?" questioned Jesse.

"Don't worry," Rip replied, sniffing the air. "One thing I am sure of: somebody left a cinnamon bun on that counter. I'll climb up and you get ready to catch it."

That's when they heard the sound every mouse dreads . . .

"Me-eeeeoowwww . . ."

Jesse let out a terrified squeal and tightly clutched her doll Bunny.

"Be brave, be brave," Rip repeated to himself. He peeked around the corner and saw a kitten crying pitifully. Despite all he had been taught about cats being his enemy, Rip found himself a claw's length from the sobbing kitten.

"Exc-c-cuse me," Rip stammered. "M-m-my n-name is Rip Squeak."

The kitten looked at Rip with startled eyes. It was too late for Rip to worry he might look like a snack to her.

"I'm Abbey. My family left without me and I'm all alone," she meowed woefully.

Rip said soothingly, "You're not alone, Abbey. My sister, Jesse and I– Hey, are you hungry?"

Jesse shrieked, "Rip, we're her **FOOD**!"

Quickly, Rip added, "I know where there's a cinnamon bun. We could share it with you."

"Oh, I love cinnamon buns!" Abbey exclaimed.

Suddenly Jesse was by Rip's side. "Then you won't eat us?"

"Of course not!" Abbey looked shocked at the idea. "I would never eat my friends!"

After breakfast, Abbey licked her paws and stated, "I've got an idea. I'll show you the garden."

"We've never been there," Rip and Jesse answered excitedly.

"Isn't that a dangerous place for mice?" questioned Jesse.

"You'll be safe with me," Abbey reassured them as she lowered herself to the ground.

"Climb aboard and I'll give you a ride."

Rip and Jesse hesitated– but only for a moment– and then crawled on up.

"What a view!" Rip exclaimed, as they raced to the garden at the speed of kitten.

Once there, they had great fun telling stories and chasing butterflies.

"You will have to meet Euripides," Abbey told them.

"Is Euripides a cat like you?" Rip wanted to know.

Abbey smiled. "Just wait," she said, and added mysteriously, "He lives at the pond."

Suddenly the sky turned dark, and it began to rain. "Meeting Euripides will have to wait until tomorrow," Abbey declared, as she safely transported the rain-soaked mice back to the cottage.

"I love the rain," Jesse announced.

"Not me!" said both Rip and Abbey, as they shook the raindrops off their heads.

Rip changed his wet clothes and found Abbey waiting for him in the sunroom.

"Where's Jesse?" he asked.

Abbey pointed out the window. Jesse was twirling her umbrella, happy to be back outside in the rain puddles.

"Can you tell me who Euripides is now?" questioned Rip.

"Tomorr– uh, oh!" Abbey gasped as her fur stood straight up. Rip followed her gaze. Two cold glowing eyes looked out from the bushes and directly at Jesse! Rip frantically banged on the window, but Jesse was lost in her rain dance. She didn't see or hear a thing as the giant yellow tomcat slinked towards her.

Without warning, the strangest thing happened. A creature wearing a big hat and cape appeared out of nowhere and pulled Jesse in next to him. He swung his sword at the vicious beast.

Abbey joined them, trying her best to look twice her size and three times as tough as the intruder. She arched her back and hissed ferociously.

"Scat!" Rip yelled as loud as he could.

Then Jesse surprised everyone! She grabbed her fallen umbrella and poked the evil-eyed monster right in the nose!

Totally confused, the enemy cat turned tail and ran.

"He almost got me, but I fought back!" Jesse said excitedly as she raced to her big brother.

"You sure did!" Rip agreed, as he hugged her close.

"We're heroes," Jesse proclaimed.

"All for one and one for all," the new friend declared.

"Let me introduce myself," he said with a bow. "Call me Eur-ribbit-ribbit-ribbit—"

He frowned and tried again. "Call me Eur-ribbit-ribbit—"

He cleared his throat and said, "Pardon me a moment. An actor must constantly practice the art of speaking clearly." His tongue began to flutter and his throat began to vibrate. "Frrreckled frrrogs frrrolic frrreely," he recited over and over. "Frrreckled frrrogs frrrolic frrreely." Finally he nodded and grinned.

"Call me Euripides!"

"Abbey, are you going to introduce your friends?" he asked.

"This is Rip and Jesse," she stated proudly.

"I've never met an actor before," Rip confessed as he stepped forward to shake the strange frog's hand.

"Well, there is a first time for everything, Rip. I don't know about you, but I think we have earned some tea. There is nothing like a hot cup of chamomile to soothe the nerves after such an ordeal."

They sat together on the kitchen counter, sipping tea and listening to Euripides tell stories about his life as an actor. When they had all recovered from their scare, Euripides pronounced, "You are a wonderful audience, but I must be off to the theater."

"It's still raining," Rip reminded him.

"Ah, my dear boy, the show must go on."

As Euripides made his exit, Abbey called after him, "What will we do for the rest of the day?"

"Use your imagination! Improvise!" Euripides shouted.

"What's improvise?" Rip asked.

"Why, it's simply making the most of an unexpected situation," he answered and vanished out the cat door.

"What do you think about having popcorn for lunch? Is that a way to impro-improvise?" Jesse wondered.

"It's a start," Abbey and Rip agreed.

So they popped popcorn, told silly jokes and laughed so hard it hurt. They played a game of hide and seek. When it was Abbey's turn to hide, Rip and Jesse could not find her anywhere. Then they heard a melancholy sound coming from the living room. They found Abbey gingerly pressing the keys of the piano with her paws.

"What's wrong, Abbey?" Rip asked.

"Oh, Rip, I miss my family!" Abbey forlornly replied.

Rip wanted to cheer her up. "Please don't stop playing, Abbey. If you play a little faster, the piano will make a happy sound and maybe that will make you happy too."

Abbey's music drew Mr. and Mrs. Squeak into the living room. The lively sound of the piano seemed to cheer Abbey up. Then there came a loud **THUMP** from the kitchen. Everyone froze, all eyes on the kitchen door.

"You must get that cat door fixed," Euripides said, rubbing his backside as he entered the room. "Continue playing, my sweet girl. The matinee was a great success and I feel like singing happy songs!"

"I really don't know any other songs," Abbey protested.

Euripides stroked his silky bow tie thoughtfully. "Continue what you were doing and we will– we will improvise, of course."

He sprang onto the piano and leaned against the sheet music on the stand. Rip wanted to join him, so he clambered over the keys, making an awful racket.

Euripides smiled at Rip, nodded at Mr. and Mrs. Squeak and winked at Jesse cuddled next to Abbey on the bench. "Just play, darling Abigail, and I'll wing it."

As Abbey began to play again, Euripides threw back his head and let out a booming operatic voice. No one understood the foreign words he sang, but the sound was beautiful. Rip danced on the keys. Abbey giggled and followed along with him. Their new tune didn't sound half-bad!

"Lovely harmony!" Euripides encouraged. "That's the spirit, dear friends!"

They danced and sang while a joyful Abbey played. In the midst of all their merriment, Abbey lifted her paws off of the keyboard. The sudden silence caught Rip in mid-step and Euripides in mid-note. Everyone looked at her questioningly. Grinning from ear to ear, Abbey excitedly exclaimed, "I've got an idea!"

"I have a surprise for you," announced Abbey.

"A surprise?" questioned Euripides. "Then I must change into something more appropriate for a surprise."

When Euripides returned, everyone wanted to know, "What are you this time?"

"Why, I'm a harlequin, of course."

"A Whataquin?" Jesse asked.

"A harlequin. A jester. A fool. A clown," Euripides explained. "And I am ready to go off on Abbey's adventure."

"All aboard," called Abbey, "and hold on tight." She bounded up the stairs, stopping in front of a closed door.

"This is it!" she declared. Abbey let off her passengers and pushed open the door with one grand sweep of her tail.

Rip, Jesse and Euripides could not believe their eyes.

"Great galloping grasshoppers!" Euripides declared.

"Oh, my," Jesse breathed in wonder.

"It's like my birthday!" Rip blurted gleefully.

"It's everyone's birthday!" Euripides agreed. "This is indeed a great adventure, Rip."

"Since we met Abigail and you, every minute feels like an adventure," he responded.

Abbey sang out, "You are the best friends— no, you're the best family anybody could wish for!"

"Let's do some exploring," encouraged Rip, heading toward a shiny train engine.

Jesse teased, "This marionette looks a lot like you, Euripides. Did you already know about this place?"

He laughed. "Just play, my friends. Life is full of mysterious things, coincidence and unanswered questions."

"Look at me," yelled Abbey, as she tried to balance herself on a ball.

"We've discovered a whole new world," exclaimed Rip, "and to think it was right under our noses the entire time!"

They played until they were too tired to play anymore. The new best friends wandered into the sunroom where Abbey contentedly plopped down on a plump pillow for a catnap. Euripides, Jesse, Bunny and Rip nestled against her, and the sound of her soft purring lulled them into sleep. As Rip's eyes grew heavier, he realized this day had changed everything.

And when he began to dream, he dreamed of the adventures tomorrow would bring.